THE PRESIDENT'S ROOM

D1124934

CHARCO PRESS

First published by Charco Press 2017

Charco Press Ltd., Office 59, 44-46 Morningside Road, Edinburgh EH10 4BF

A CIP catalogue record for this book is available from the British Library.

ISBN: 978 1 9997227 2 2
e-book: 978 1 9997227 3 9

www.charcopress.com

Edited by Annie McDermott
Cover design by Pablo Font
Typeset by Laura Jones

Printed in Glasgow by Bell and Bain using responsibly sourced paper and
environmentally-friendly adhesive

Ricardo Romero

THE PRESIDENT'S ROOM

Translated by Charlotte Coombe

CHARCO PRESS

For Victoria, on her birthday,
this and all stories.

Or, to put it another way,
is it possible that the secret
lies open before us,
that we already know what it is?

STEVEN MILLHAUSER, 'THE SISTERHOOD OF NIGHT'

The house isn't big, but it's not small either, compared to the rest of the houses on the block. It has two floors, three if you count the attic, a storage room up on the roof terrace where nobody goes apart from me. The rest of the family call it the loft, but I prefer to call it the attic. I didn't decide this on a whim. It's something I've thought about a lot, up there in the attic, among the old furniture, the trunks, and always the same warmish air capturing the rays of sun as they filter through the skylight and the frosted glass of the door. Rays of sun, skylight, frosted glass. When I'm there, I'm able to think 'I'm in the attic', but I find it impossible to think 'I'm in the loft'. Not everything can be thought. Why should everything have to be thinkable?

On the first floor of the house are the bedrooms. My parents' room, my older brother's room and the one I share with my younger brother. There are two large bathrooms that seem much older than the rest of the house, as if they've always been there, hovering at the height of the first floor, waiting for my family to come and build the house around them. The bathtubs, the taps and the medicine cabinet are majestic; the porcelain, mirror and brass are yellowing in the corners with stains that aren't stains, because you can get rid of a stain but you can't get rid of these. I can't imagine the tap in our bathroom sink without that pale, discoloured cloud underneath it, or the mirror of the medicine cabinet in my parents' bathroom without the black spots on the left-hand side. However, what really makes these bathrooms feel old, as if they're of an earlier time, are the tiles covering the walls

1

right up to the ceiling. What is it that makes those tiles so old? I don't know. I only know that they're impossible to count. No, that's not all I know. I also know that although the bathrooms seem the same, like twins, they're not.

And then there's the ground floor, which is the same size as the first but seems bigger. It only seems it, though: I know they're really the same size. And yet, even though I know this, every now and again I feel the need to compare corners and angles, to see how the walls of one floor and another are the same. Or rather: are aligned. The walls of the ground floor and those of the first floor are aligned. However, the ground floor seems bigger.

On the ground floor are the kitchen, the dining room, the living room and the study my father shares with my older brother. There's another, smaller bathroom, squeezed in between the kitchen and the staircase. There's a small cleaning cupboard. There's an entrance hall leading to the front door.

And of course, at the front of the house on the left, looking out over the garden, is the president's room.

The staircase. The grand staircase where my younger brother plays. Which floor is it on? The ground floor, or the first floor? Although that's not the right question to ask, because I could easily answer that it's on the ground floor. So, the right question to ask is: which floor does it belong to? This is harder to answer. Does it belong to the ground floor or the first floor? Could the exact location of the staircase be what makes one floor seem larger than the other? Could it hold the key to this distortion that I imagine but can't see?

If the bathrooms are the oldest part of the house, the president's room is the newest. But it's new in the way the bathrooms are old. My grandparents built this house before the neighbourhood was a neighbourhood. Now there are barely any empty spaces left and the houses are crowded together side by side. But I don't want to think about that. About the houses stuck to one another. When my grandparents were building the house, the president's room came before the bathrooms, which is obvious, because how could they have built the bathrooms first if there was nothing below them?

Our bathroom, the bathroom I share with my brothers, is directly over the president's room. When we pull the flush, can he hear it below us? Can he hear the noise of the shower or the silence when we're masturbating? So as not to think about it, not to think about the president when I'm in the bathroom, I try to count the tiles. But there are just too many.

There's no basement. None of the houses in the neighbourhood have one. They've been banned since my grandparents were around. People say that terrible things used to happen before, in the basements. That's why no more basements were allowed to be built. In the houses dating back to the times before the ban, the basements were bricked up. Although they're large houses, they're cheap nowadays, easy to buy. People don't like living in those houses. It's understandable. Who'd want to live above a sealed room, devoid of all light?

From the window of the room I share with my younger brother, we can see the street. The small front garden, the little metal gate with its peeling white paint, the pavement and the street. On the pavement right opposite our house, there's a tall laurel tree, with a lot of dark leaves. My brother, who's still little, sometimes climbs it. I'll be sitting at my desk, doing my homework, and when I look up I see him tucked away among the branches. At first, without fail, I always think he's spying on me. But then I realise that it's not me he's spying on. He's spying on the president's room. So then I wave at him, but he doesn't wave back. I know my parents talk about him more than they do about my older brother and me. And when they do, they do it in hushed tones. They're worried. For some reason, they seem to prefer to do it in the kitchen. As if that were the place in the house for talking about those things that need to be talked about in hushed tones. They talk about my little brother more, and they talk to my older brother more. I'm the middle child and I'm always in the middle. Conversations aren't normally directed at me. I don't mind. It means I can do things like go to the attic and nobody will disturb me for hours.

Nobody knows, or at least I don't think anybody knows, but I've also climbed the laurel tree to peer into the president's room. Right now, I'm not doing that. Right now, as I'm sitting at my desk and looking at the laurel tree from my bedroom window, I'm wondering what the tree looks like from the president's room.

Since long before basements were banned, people were building rooms for the president. Every house has one. Or at least houses owned by people like us. The blocks of flats in the city centre don't. And because they don't, they lose their privileges. I don't really know what those privileges are, or even whether our parents know what they are, but nobody doubts that they exist. In our neighbourhood, all the houses have a president's room. And yet the president has never been to visit us. It's not that we're expecting him, because to be honest, most of the time we forget the room's even there. Most of the time, we forget.

When I said the president had never come to our neighbourhood, that wasn't entirely true. Our school is in our neighbourhood, and the president visited a boy from our school once. Or at least, that's what people say. Everyone says it, because there's not much else to say about the president, although nobody dares to ask the boy, who is slightly older than me, if it's true. The boy lives in a different neighbourhood but he goes to our school, like lots of children from other neighbourhoods. That's normal. It's a big school, and there aren't enough children in our neighbourhood to fill it. And a school should be full.

We're not jealous of him. The boy's no different to any of us. There's nothing about him to make us think he's special, or that his family's different. He walks around the playground with his tie loose and his sleeves rolled up, he laughs and gets angry as quickly as any of us. He's tall and skinny and always well-groomed. He is pale. But then, lots of us are pale. Sometimes I bump into him in the toilets and he's always slicking his hair back with a comb he keeps in his back pocket. I've never dared talk to him because he's older than me. But I've heard him talking to boys his age, and he doesn't seem to stand out for any particular reason. He laughs at anything, gets angry at anything, nudges his friends when one of the pretty girls walks past. Like my friends and I do. I don't know why, but at school we're all like that. We act as if we were younger, as if we enjoyed being with other people, even though when we're alone at home we're overwhelmed by an anxiety that makes us want to hide away, to be even more alone. I don't know where the others hide, where the boy the president visited hides, but I hide in the attic.

There's no proof and nobody's asked him about it, but I'm sure what people say is true: that the president went to the boy's house. At school events or when the headmistress is making her speeches, at moments when we all have to be quiet and pay attention, I've seen him, I've watched him, and I'm certain that while we're all sitting there, bored stiff, our minds wandering, he's thinking only about one thing. He's thinking about the president. There's a worried look on his face, as if it's suddenly become the face of an adult. Because he's thinking about the president a lot, much more than we are.

The house changes at night. Sometimes, I walk around it while my family are sleeping. The change has nothing to do with the darkness, or with the temperature. It's as if the house changes its relationship to what's outside it, and so being inside means something else. I press my ear against the walls, the doors, the floors, the terrace. I walk barefoot. I never go into the president's room.

There are, in the house, at night, more inhabitants than there are during the day.

But it does have something to do with the darkness, and it does have something to do with the temperature. More with the temperature than with the darkness. The first floor is a more pleasant temperature than the ground floor. It's always colder in the corners of the rooms than in the middle. The warmest place of all is the attic. On the stairs, the air is always still.

That's during the day. During the night, the only temperature in the house is that of my body.

The laurel tree in front of our house is tall and leafy. Every time someone comes to visit us for the first time, they tell us it's the tallest laurel they have ever seen. It's been there since before they built the house, since before the neighbourhood was even a neighbourhood. Just like in the attic, inside its foliage the rays of sunlight become visible. I know this because I used to climb it, though now I don't. Now I go to the attic. Or the terrace. Because there are times when I don't go into the attic and I stay on the terrace, looking at the roofs of the neighbouring houses, the tops of the trees on the block, the motorways on the horizon and the buildings in the centre, an approaching storm or the cloudless sky. When there are no clouds, there's so much light that it's as if I can't breathe. The afternoon sun bounces off the white floor of the terrace, blinding me. The only thing I can see then is the top of the laurel tree appearing several feet above. Dark. And the question arises, and I panic a little. I imagine myself taking a run-up and jumping, trying to reach the laurel tree and falling with my arms open wide. However hard I try, whether with my eyes shut or with them half-closed, squinting against the sun's glare, I can never imagine myself reaching it. I can never imagine myself landing on the branches. The question goes unanswered and I'm left feeling slightly dizzy, sensing that I was about to feel something new. What I can feel is me hitting the pavement. A dry thud that judders and stuns. Like when my grandfather used to spank us. But my grandfather's no longer here and the laurel tree is.

When the afternoon sky is very blue and I'm out on the terrace, I can hear music. It's being played by someone, one or more people, on real instruments. I haven't managed to work out where it comes from, which house, or who's making it or listening to it. It drifts in when the breeze drops, mingling with the sounds of the city, which are fewer than you might think. It comes from far away. The city's far away. It's like the city's always somewhere else. There's always a moment when all you can hear is the music, trembling alone in the air, and that's the exact moment before it disappears.

My little brother has a fever again. He's been in bed since yesterday. Right behind me, all wrapped up, watching as I sit writing at my desk. 'What are you writing?' he asks. 'I'm writing that while I'm writing you're watching me write', I say without turning around. 'I'm not watching you', he replies. I turn around and see him watching me, his eyes wide and shining with fever. If we were good brothers, we'd both laugh at this point. But we're not good brothers. We don't laugh together. I can't remember if we've ever laughed together, at the same time. We never give each other the giggles, any more than we give each other our illnesses. My big brother doesn't count, because he doesn't laugh or get ill.

Before my brother started getting bouts of fever, it was my grandfather who used to suffer from them. The difference is that my grandfather would get angry. He would never let anybody near him. He would shout. He would talk to himself, cursing and swearing. My little brother, on the other hand, stays quiet most of the time. He spends days like that, until the fever leaves as suddenly as it came. My little brother never knew our grandfather, but when I see him like that, wrapped up in his blankets, glassy eyes staring fixedly at a point on the ceiling, I think what he's doing is listening to our grandfather. He's listening to him shouting and talking to himself, he's hearing him swearing and cursing. One of them is alive and the other is dead, but they both have a fever.

My mother is the one who goes into the president's room the most often. Naturally, because she's the one who cleans the house; the one who cleans the room. Once a week she goes in and cleans, and while she's in there she leaves the door slightly ajar. When she's finished, the door stays slightly open like that for a few hours so the floor can dry, because my mother prefers not to open the window. That's when the lurking begins. My younger brother and I find any excuse to walk past the door and peek inside. It's not that we're forbidden from going in, but if we went in and were found out, we'd be subjected to the inevitable questioning, and we both want to avoid that. The long, tedious interrogations during which our parents look at one another every time we answer, and take notes (my father's the one who writes the notes). Whatever answer we give, there's always a seriousness to those occasions that scares us. It's impossible to tell what we've done wrong. It's impossible to tell if we've done anything wrong. There are never any consequences. So we stick to lurking, sneaking glimpses of the sliver of room we can see through the crack in the door. The same bookcase with the same books and objects on it, the edge of a desk, the coat stand in the corner, always bare. Nothing very interesting. Nothing new in the way things are arranged. And yet, once a week, every time our mother cleans the president's room, my little brother and I succumb to temptation. We lurk. And at the same time, we avoid each other. This means we're spying on each other as well as lurking. The spying is unnecessary, seeing as we're not even there for the same reason. My brother is attracted to the things that have been accumulating in the president's room since the time of my grandfather. What attracts me is the room itself. The desire to see it without furniture or ornaments. The president's room just as it was in the beginning.

When our mother finally closes the door, my brother and I, wherever we are, breathe a sigh of relief.

We know the objects in the president's room off by heart. We even know the order in which they arrived there. The desk, the wooden recliner, the camp bed in one corner. These were the first things my grandfather brought. My grandmother provided the sheets and the blankets. The mat for the doorway. Then my grandfather brought the lamp for the desk, the coat stand and the two bookcases. My grandmother started putting some books in there. Some ornaments. My grandfather added a small table for drinks in one corner, along with some whisky glasses and a bottle. An enormous ceramic ashtray my grandmother broke one time when she was cleaning and then mended with glue. In the drawers of the desk there are matches, cigarettes, a large and a small coffee cup, packets of sugar, a comb, a toothbrush, some little nail scissors, tissues, two handkerchiefs, various packs of cards and a book of crosswords.

There are more things. Many more things that we don't know about. But when we think about it, we always think that yes, we know them all off by heart, we know exactly how each object got there.

My father went through an enthusiastic phase when he put things in the room, particularly books, the kind he likes, about science. My mother never did. For as long as I can remember, only one other member of the family has added anything new. It was my older brother. One breakfast-time, before we set off for school, my big brother, without looking up from his cup of milky coffee, said he wanted to put something in the president's room. No, he didn't say that.

He said something else. He was twelve and his head looked too big for his body. 'I've got something for the president,' he said. Those were his words. My parents looked at one another in silence. 'What have you got?' my mother asked. My brother went up to the room that all three of us shared at the time and came back with a magnifying glass. Quite a large magnifying glass with a wooden handle. My parents said we could talk about it over dinner, all of us, and then we went off to school. That evening we did the little ritual. The ritual was this: everyone in the house, including my younger brother and me, who were still too little to understand what was going on, had to agree on the item. Then we all had to imagine what things the president could do with it. It was a fun task that lasted a long time. It was one of the few times we laughed together. Finally, when we'd exhausted all the possibilities, my older brother went into the president's room and chose a place for the magnifying glass. He put it on one of the shelves of the bookcase, next to a row of elephants of different sizes. The elephants got bigger as they got closer to the magnifying glass. At the time I didn't understand why, but I didn't like the spot my older brother chose. I thought it seemed too prominent. But that's the way my older brother is. I, on the other hand, would have kept it in a desk drawer. I would have hidden it among the handkerchiefs, for example. But that's the way I am. Anyway, I can't really talk, because although I've tried many times, I've never found anything I wanted to put in the president's room.

Perhaps the difference is that my older brother brought the magnifying glass for the president, whereas I've always been looking for an object for the president's room. I know this seems like it could be the same thing, but it's not. There's an abyss in there that swallows up all the objects I've ever considered. They disappear into that void. But I don't think about it too much because I know that if I did, I'd fall in too.

My brother's fever has lasted longer this time. All the talking he doesn't do while he's awake, he does while he's asleep. You can't make out what he's saying, but he's saying something. Is he pretending to have a fever, my younger brother? Probably. Fever can never be entirely real.

I've only once been in a house that used to have a basement. It was the birthday of a friend from school. There were lots of us there and we were making plenty of noise, but I'm sure none of us failed to notice the presence of this closed-off room. Behind one of the walls, a staircase led down into the darkness. We played together, shyly trying to get the girls' attention. But everything we said, all our boisterous laughter, was insignificant. The echo was different. The echo was significant. Our voices reached the black interior of that sealed room and bounced back against the unknown.

Blocks of flats aren't banned like basements are, but that doesn't mean they're considered acceptable. There are some that have so many upper floors that the floors below become something completely different. And terrible things can start to happen. They say the ground is for the dead and the air is for the living. So who are those flats for, those buried flats, entombed in the air?

My younger brother doesn't have a fever any more. Now I'm the one with a fever. I haven't said anything to my parents. I think my mother's noticed, but because I'm not saying anything she's not saying anything either. It's not a very high fever and it just comes over me at dusk, when I'm in the attic. During the day it's like an atmosphere that surrounds me, as if the fever were outside me rather than inside. It's not the first time this has happened to me. And it's not the first time that having a fever has meant I do things I normally wouldn't dare to do. Once I told the girl I like that I liked her. She laughed, but ever since then I've been able to tell that she likes me. That she's looking at me. Yesterday I was in the toilets at school, splashing water on my burning face, when the boy they say the president visited came in. He wet his face too, and his hair, and then got out his comb and combed his hair. We looked at one another in the mirror and I said 'Hi'. The boy said 'Hi' and carried on combing his hair. I'd finished washing my face and had to go, but I didn't. I stayed there, looking at myself in the mirror. My eyes were shining with fever. I looked pale and exhausted. When I went out into the playground I looked for the girl I like, but I couldn't find her.

$\mathbf{A}$m I thinking about things that upset me because my fever's worsening, or is my fever worsening because I'm thinking about things that upset me? I'm sitting on the floor in the attic, leaning against an old bedside table that smells musty. I can feel the cold sweat, the tightness in my skin. I wrap myself in a blanket and tell myself that I'm not going to think about the adjoining walls, but that just makes me think about them. A house shouldn't touch another house. At least not all the time. Is it possible to live like that? Sometimes from my bedroom I can hear the noises the neighbours make. There's nothing stranger or more terrifying than that. Feverishly, I think: houses shouldn't be touching all the time. I don't know what shape our house is. I don't know what shape my body is, my body that's always touching something. As I think this, I shudder.

Has the president ever been ill? The president is in the news and on the TV every day. He's a tall man, very tall and slightly hunchbacked. He must be about seventy, and he walks slowly and talks slowly. His suits all look the same, they're all blue or grey and my mother thinks they always look too big on him. His ties usually vary, though. The president is in the news every day, but they never say if he's visited anybody. That's never part of the news. He has a big face, the president, and when I was little it used to scare me. Not now. His nose looks like a potato, and my mother says that's why he has a moustache. To hide it a bit. We know what colour his eyes are, but we don't know what it's like when they look at you, because, of course, he never looks at the camera.

The fever is in my skin. The fever is my skin and it's multiplying it. Skin. My skin. When I have a fever, I can feel my skin, it feels right, and then I wonder: does my skin always belong to me or is it sometimes part of what's in the air, what's outside and around me? It's like the walls, the adjacent, adjoining walls. It hurts me to think about it. It hurts me not knowing which house a wall belongs to. And the whole city's like that, full of walls that belong to two houses at once. My temperature soars. My skin is burning. I touch my face and the skin of my face doesn't recognise the skin of my hands. My skin is a wall and I don't know what's on one side and what's on the other.

My fever has gone and although I feel better, I've been left with an echo of those days. Thoughts that confuse me. In the attic, during siesta, I can't help trying to imagine what it's like to live in one of the blocks of flats in the city centre where nobody has a president's room. It's not just the walls that are adjoining, but also the ceilings and floors. So, the apartment below is a basement for the one above? And the one above is an attic for the one below? Is there a point in the day when the inhabitants no longer know, are no longer sure, which floor they're on? Or which way is up and which way is down? Thinking about this confuses me, but it's not an entirely unpleasant feeling.

The girl I like hasn't been at school for over a month. I realised the other day when I looked for her, when I had a fever and wanted to talk to her. For over two years now I've liked her, and for over two years I've spied on her at break time. Her friends told me she had to go away because of some family problem. How did I not notice? Who have I been looking at all this time?

My grandfather died after I was born. The room my older brother has now used to belong to my grandfather. I don't have many memories of him, and those I do have don't come to me when I want them to. They come of their own accord and then go away again. They're memories full of big things, big things that cast big shadows. Because when you're little, you're closer to shadows than you are to things. Sometimes when I hear sounds coming from my older brother's room, I think for a moment that it's my grandfather making those sounds. Sometimes I think my older brother is my grandfather. He says that one night, while I was asleep, I went into his room and talked to him as if I were talking to my grandfather. I'm not sure whether this is true or not. I don't know if I ever talked to my grandfather, if I'd even learnt how to talk before he died. What would I say to my grandfather? I can't think of anything. I can't think of anything to say to my older brother either. A few hours ago I felt the urge to speak to him, so I went looking for him. He was in the study he shares with my father, bent over his books and frowning. I asked him what he was studying. At first, he was surprised. He blushed. There's not so much of an age gap between us, but you only notice that when we talk, on the rare occasions when we talk. Then he started telling me what he was reading. I tried to follow, but I got lost. He was talking about some law of physics. That's what my brother's studying. Physics. I nodded every now and again. I raised my eyebrows. And although I couldn't understand any of what he was explaining to me, I was sincere. My older brother knows a lot of things. I even think he even knows more things than my grandfather knew. My grandfather was a man of few words, my mother said once. Sometimes this seems like praise, and other times like a reproach. My older brother has plenty of words but he never says them. That's praise. It's also a reproach. When he finished his explanation, he looked worn out. I knew I should say something nice, so I did. My older brother smiled. 'The laws of physics are invisible,' I said, even though it had nothing to do with anything. My older brother raised his eyebrows and told me I was right. At that moment, I felt like I was the grandfather and he was the grandson. I felt old and distant. Is there some law of physics behind these transformations? Later, when my older brother had gone to his university seminars, I went into the study and leafed through one of his books. I spent a long time turning the pages, reading the odd paragraph, looking at the diagrams and illustrations. I understood a little more after that. But not much.

When I'm in the bathroom, I sometimes imagine that I'll open the door and there'll be no house there, just a void. The bathroom floating in the air, before the house was a house. Nearby there'll be the other bathroom, and further away the laurel tree. At first, imagining this gives me a kind of pleasure I can't understand. Then I feel upset, but have no idea why. The only way out, then, is to close my eyes, open the door and take the first step.

Our president wasn't always the president. There were others before him, and there will be others after him. In some houses – I know because my friends at school have told me – people put up pictures of the dead presidents in the president's room. My mother thinks this is in poor taste. She says nothing good can come of the president seeing his predecessors right there in front of him. I don't know what to think. Because it's so hard to know what the president would do if he ever went into the room. I'd like to ask the boy from school. They say that something went wrong in his house, and that for quite a while afterwards he had a fearful look about him. They say he got skinnier and paler, wouldn't look you in the eye and seemed to be searching for something in the corners of rooms. But there are a lot of things that can look like fear. And there's a lot to see in corners.

My younger brother has disappeared again. Sometimes he has a fever, other times he disappears. My parents, my big brother and I always go out looking for him in the neighbourhood. We know that he's on his bike, and that he's probably thinking about other things, and that's why he hasn't come back. He pedals and gets lost, and when we find him, several hours after dark, he greets us as if he'd been the one looking for us. We're about to set off. We'll have to take torches with us. My father and I will go on foot. My older brother and our mother will take the car. My older brother will drive. The last time my younger brother disappeared it took us several hours to find him. He was cycling down the middle of a street lined with trees so tall they formed a canopy at the top, blocking out the light from the street-lamps. He was zigzagging along, getting gradually further away. He wasn't in a hurry. We saw him turn a corner and my father shouted out his name. He turned around, and when he recognised us he made a U-turn and pedalled towards us. He was smiling radiantly. My feet hurt from walking so far. It was very late and my father seemed angry this time. He didn't say anything to him, though. He didn't say much at all. He just told him off for not letting us know where he was. And I thought: that's not a telling-off. If you're going to disappear or go out and get lost, you're not going to let people know beforehand. He should have been told off for something else entirely. For example, I wanted to tell him that he'd made me miss my favourite TV programme.

This time, my father and I spent hours walking on our

own through the neighbourhood. On the industrial estate, dogs barked at us. One even howled, it sounded like it was crying. I distracted myself by trying to imagine where the president's room might be located in each of the houses we saw. A couple of times we spotted our car driving past, one or two blocks away. It was moving slowly, very slowly. You couldn't see my older brother or my mother. It was as if the car was going along of its own accord. It looked like it was about to stop at any moment, but it never did.

Generally, the president's room is on the ground floor of a house, near the front door. It usually has a window looking out onto the street. The room might be on the right or left-hand side of the house, it doesn't matter which. What seems important is for it to be near the front door, though it's not clear whether this is so the president can find it easily, or so that he doesn't go beyond that room, into other rooms that aren't his. Is it always easy for the president to tell which room is his? From the street, without knowing the houses, it's hard to guess which window belongs to the president's room.

My mother says it's not good to put photos of the dead presidents in the president's room. But I know, and everyone in our house knows, that at the very back of the right-hand drawer of the desk, there's a revolver.

Did I ever talk to my grandfather? I remember the sound of his smacks more than I remember his voice. It wasn't me he smacked, I was very little then. It was my older brother, who's now the owner of his room.

There are nights, those nights when I walk through the house in the dark while everyone's sleeping, when I hear the smacking. I lean against the door of my big brother's room and hear the smacking. An unmistakeable cracking sound.

This time, we didn't find my little brother. We went back home. My mother wanted to call the police but my father wouldn't let her. I hardly ever saw my father forbid anyone from doing anything. They were worried, we were all worried, though I'm not sure if we were all worrying about the same thing. My mother locked herself in the bathroom and cried. I could hear her as I lay in bed, waiting for the dawn. Was she crying because my younger brother hadn't turned up, or because she was tired? And if she was crying because she was tired, was it because she was tired of my younger brother doing things like this or just because she was tired? I couldn't sleep either. I thought about going up to the attic, but when I looked out of the window of our bedroom and saw the enormous figure of the laurel tree in the night, I had the urge to climb it instead. I dressed without making a sound, then went down the stairs and out of the house. I climbed up the laurel tree. As I went, I realised my body had grown. My arms were pulling me up more easily, but there was less space among the branches and it was hard to find a comfortable position. I stayed there, looking towards the end of the road, with the roofs of the warehouses a few streets away and, further on, the line of the motorway and the blocks of flats in the city centre on the horizon. This sight made me drowsy. I have no idea how long I slept, but I woke up suddenly, about to topple off the branch I was resting on. I grabbed hold of the branch and, once the shock had passed, looked in the direction of the house.

I didn't think about the president's room until I looked through the window and saw the silhouette of a man in the armchair. He was sideways-on, raising a glass to his mouth. My heart stopped. 'The president!' I thought. But then I realised it wasn't the president. It was my father. My father, sitting in the president's armchair, drinking the president's whisky. Everything was in darkness. My father was my father and he was also a dark, motionless silhouette. I didn't want to see it, and yet I couldn't stop looking. My father. A stranger. The stranger wasn't looking out of the window but rather at something inside the dark room. Clinging onto the branch, I wondered if the stranger had seen me climbing the laurel tree. I felt ashamed. I missed my father. Every so often, the stranger raised the glass to his lips. I looked for my father in this single gesture, but I didn't find him. Where could my father be, where could my little brother be? I wondered this and I also wondered if I'd be a stranger to this stranger if he happened to look out of the window and see me. My neck hurt and I could feel my muscles straining. I could feel my muscles. The stranger suddenly stood up and moved out of sight. I saw the light in the hallway as he opened the door of the president's room and walked through it. I climbed back down the laurel tree and went into the house. My father was walking up the stairs, and he turned to look at me.

My little brother appeared at dawn, while we were all sleeping. Nobody heard him come back, pedalling his bike, with his beaming smile, as if he'd been looking for us and had just found us. I didn't hear him come into the room or get into bed. But when I woke up, there he was. He slept all day. Our parents talked a lot in the kitchen, in very low voices. It was a day of relief but also of furtive glances. Since that day, I've never seen the stranger again. Sometimes I still miss my father.

What could have gone wrong in the boy's house when the president visited? Was there something in the room that shouldn't have been there? What did the president do and how long did he stay? This is what we do. To avoid thinking about what the president would do if he came to visit us, we think about what he did when he visited that boy.

The president always smiles wearily at the cameras. His voice is thick and dry, and every so often he clears his throat. If he did ever come, I'd like to ask him what he thinks of adjoining walls, of houses stuck to one another. I'd also like to ask him if he prefers the word *attic* or the word *loft*.

Where do the people who live in the city centre, the people who live in blocks of flats that don't have rooms for the president, keep the things for the president? Where do they keep the thoughts they have about those things and about that room they don't have? We don't think about the president's room much. We think about it just the right amount, as much as we think about any other part of the house.

When I think about a place, I'm usually in another place. But I think about the attic only when I'm in the attic.

The boy the president visited had a fight this morning with one of his best friends. It was during first break, when it's still cold and you can see your breath steaming in the air when you're in the playground. It's hard to know who won, because they both ended up with blood on them. Neither of them cried. Neither of them surrendered. The fight, of course, was over a girl. 'Over which girl?' I asked. They told me her name. I didn't know her and nobody could point her out at the next break time. The school is very, very big.

The best friend of the boy the president visited was picked up by his parents. Nobody came to pick up the boy the president visited.

At night, I go downstairs barefoot. At night, I go upstairs barefoot. How many times have I done that? How many nights? And yet, I swear, I wasn't expecting what happened to happen.

I was sitting halfway down the stairs, not really wanting to go all the way to the bottom but not wanting to go back up either. I was thinking about the girl I liked, who I haven't seen again. I was looking in the direction of the hallway with its light that's always on: the only light in the house that stays on all night. The light illuminates the hallway and the front door. It was an empty scene and I was an empty spectator. Neither expected anything from the other, and that was fine. But things didn't stay like that. I heard the key first, then I saw the lock turn. Do locks always turn so slowly? The handle lowered and the door opened. A man entered, breathing heavily. He closed the door after him and turned to lock it. He wiped his sizeable feet on the doormat and cleared his throat. It was the president. I didn't move. I didn't stop breathing. I didn't stop being there. The president came in, walked through the hallway and then looked from side to side, but not towards the staircase. He ascertained that on one side there was the living room, then further on the kitchen, then he chose the door on the other side: the door to his room. He opened it, went inside and closed the door.

He was dressed just like when we see him on TV. Dark blue suit, slightly more crumpled than it looks on screen. From above, he also looked more stooped and his nose seemed darker than the rest of his face. Now and again he touched his chin or stroked his moustache.

I stayed still for a while. Expectant. Then I plucked up the courage to go downstairs. The president had turned on the light in his room; I could see it through the crack under the door. I pressed my ear against the door and listened. But I couldn't hear anything. Grabbing my mother's key from the hook, I opened the front door and went out of the house, across the garden and onto the pavement, and stopped in front of the laurel tree. I was shaking as I climbed up, and I was still shaking when I reached the top. Through the window of the president's room, I could see the president. He was standing in the middle of the room, his head down, as if examining the tips of his shoes. Occasionally he raised a hand to his face. He scratched his chin, stroked his moustache. The light fell on his grey hair and his nose in the shadows looked enormous. He looked funny, but also frightening. The president looked like he couldn't make up his mind. I felt the urge to help him, but I couldn't think how. He stayed there a long time, a very long time. Then he turned around, switched off the light and left the room. A few seconds later I saw him go out of the house and disappear hastily up the street. His rapid footsteps on the pavement were the only thing you could hear in the night. His footsteps coupled with the beating of my heart.

Does the president have keys to all the houses or had my parents been told about his visit and somehow managed to get a key to him? The following day I had a fever and stayed at home all day. I really did have a temperature, but I was also pretending a bit. I wanted to keep an eye on my parents, to see if anything gave them away. Did they know the president had been in our house? Was it the first time it had happened? I didn't see anything that gave them away. Yesterday my mother cleaned the president's room as if nothing had happened.

What about our neighbours? Hadn't they seen or heard anything? But if I'm going to ask this, I have to ask other things as well. Can I see my neighbours, can I hear them? Can I know for sure that the president hasn't visited them? Can we, our family, vouch for the fact that the president hasn't been in their house? Our neighbours are there and we're here, and that's all we need to know about each other.

My big brother is in the study with his books. My little brother is in my big brother's room, rummaging through his things. My mother is in the kitchen making dinner. My father is in the living room watching television. I'm in my room, writing. That's all I need to know about them. That's all I need to know about myself.

Although I'm in the attic, right now it's as if I was on the staircase in the middle of the night, transfixed by the empty scene of the hallway with the closed door illuminated by the only light in the whole house. I've stayed awake for several nights now, but the president hasn't returned. I know I didn't dream it. I know the president's been in our house, in the room we've made for him. Has something gone wrong? Are my friends looking at me the way they look at the boy the president visited? The day before yesterday, yesterday and today I've been about to speak to the boy, to tell him, to ask him. The only thing holding me back is the possibility that the president didn't really go to his house. That would make *me* the boy the president visited. I don't want to become that boy.

Is that how the president goes around, alone at night, alone in the streets? Doesn't he have bodyguards or ministers who go with him? Doesn't he have a driver who takes him wherever he wants to go?

Today the president came back. He was wearing a grey suit and a dark tie. He let himself into our house with the key, and locked the door behind him. He wiped his feet on the doormat, touched his face in the light of the hallway, stroked the moustache that doesn't manage to hide his nose. The only thing he didn't do was look in the direction of the living room. He went straight into his room, and this time he didn't turn on the light. I went outside and, from the laurel tree, after peering at the dark window for a while, was able to make out his legs, crossed and outstretched on the camp bed. I couldn't see the rest of his body, only his legs and feet. Had the president taken off his shoes? Had he fallen asleep? Clinging to a branch, I awkwardly pulled myself along it to get a better view. The president was a large shadow lying on the camp bed. He had his arms folded behind his head. I stayed there, expecting something to happen, but nothing did. This time, the president stayed much longer. Suddenly I had an idea. I climbed down the laurel tree, went back into the house and tiptoed to the door of the president's room. I listened. The president was making a hissing sound. It was a musical, muffled whistling, trying to follow the cadence of a song I didn't recognise. I listened for so long, so quietly and attentively, that at a certain point I no longer knew if the president was still whistling or if the music was in my head. This scared me and I left. I don't know when the president left.

Air between the teeth, lips pressed together. That's how he whistled. Sometimes I do it deliberately, to see how my family will react, but sometimes I also do it without realising. The song is there and suddenly I realised what I'm doing. In the attic, at school, in the street. Also in the bathroom, or when I'm lying in bed trying to get to sleep.

My big brother and my little brother are talking. When I appear, they stop and look at me. The conversation is easily broken. It doesn't start again. It's not that they're hiding something from me, it's just that any change in their surroundings disrupts it. Sometimes I'll be talking to one of them, and when the other one appears we'll fall silent and look at him. I haven't told either of them that I've seen the president in our house, twice. Actually, I've told both of them when I've been alone in the attic. And then, in my imagination, our parents appear and we all fall silent and look at them.

What would my grandfather say if he knew the president had finally come? Would he be pleased, would he be scared? My grandfather was always scared. Even when he was calmly sitting in front of the TV watching his favourite programme, eyes wide and eyebrows raised, he seemed to be running away from something. He wasn't a coward, it's not that. I think it's just what happens to people who build their own houses.

The house is the same. Nothing has changed since the president came. That is, the house has changed as much as it always changes, at the edges of our awareness. It's never so noticeably mysterious that we feel threatened. It's our house. The house our grandparents built. It would be different if the house had a basement.

This time it was intentional. I went into the school toilets and, while I was peeing and then afterwards washing my hands, I whistled the song I'd heard from the president. Lips together, teeth clenched, I whistled through them. At the sink next to mine was the boy the president visited. He wet his hair and combed it in front of the mirror. My song didn't seem to get his attention. However, he started whistling as well. It was a different song, a different melody, slightly happier than mine. Could it be a code? Have we started a conversation I don't understand?

When the boy the president visited left the toilets, I stayed there alone, thoughtful. I no longer feel like he's a lot bigger than me. I'm not scared to talk to him any more. The problem is that I don't know what to say to him. I thought of asking him about the fight he had that time, but he seemed to have forgotten about it already. Him and his best friend. They go around together all the time, making fun of each other and losing their temper with each other as if nothing had happened. Up until now, I've never been in a fight with anybody, not even my brothers, so I don't know if it's something that really happens. Not a single fight, even with my brothers. The second time, I whistled the song unintentionally. There was nobody else in the toilets. The boy the president visited had gone and there was just me, the boy the president visited.

I was no longer expecting the president to come back, and yet he came back. I was convinced that those two visits would be all. That the president wasn't interested in our room, the room we had for him. He hadn't looked through the drawers or the bookcases, he hadn't used anything we'd left for him except the camp bed. On the second visit, he hadn't even switched on the light. All he did was lie down and whistle softly through his teeth. That's something he could have done anywhere. And yet he came back. Last night. The president came back to our house. This time I wasn't sitting on the staircase. I was in the kitchen, with the fridge door open, looking inside. When I heard the key in the front door, I shut the fridge and hid behind one of the living room armchairs. The president came in. Now I was at his level, and I could even see him from beneath because I was crouching down. He was wearing a navy-blue suit and a tie that was very dark red. This suit looked newer than the others, and bigger. As if the president had shrunk. The president didn't look in my direction, but oddly he looked towards the staircase, which he hadn't done before. Was he expecting me to be there? Had he seen me the previous times and pretended he hadn't? He touched his face and stroked his moustache. From where I was, in the light of the hallway, his moustache and nose were a single dark mass that seemed not to belong to the rest of his face. Another thing I discovered from this new perspective: the president, with his momentous dark nose, seemed to be sniffing, searching out a scent. What could our house smell of? Of that evening's food? Of us, our family? And what would that smell be? Just then I had an idea, but I decided to think about it later. The president had already gone into his room and I hurried outdoors. This time I didn't climb the laurel tree. This new perspective made me feel brave. I dared to stay in the garden and moved closer to the window. I wanted to see the whole room, not to miss any detail of what the president was doing. He'd switched on the light and once again was standing in the middle of the room. He was touching his face. In this light, his nose and moustache were red, like those red patches you see when you close your eyes or when you stand up suddenly and feel dizzy. The president sighed. I could hear, from the other side of the window, the air coming out of his mouth. He sighed twice. Then he sighed a third time, more deeply, lifting his shoulders and lowering them as he breathed out. But this didn't seem to satisfy him. He lifted his arms as if somebody was pointing a gun at him, and took three deep breaths in. He breathed in deeply and breathed out slowly. Then, appearing satisfied, he began to walk around the room. He circled the desk, passed the recliner, then went back to where he was before, but this time he stood with his back to the window. He thought for a few seconds. I could see his stooped shoulders rising and falling to the rhythm of his breath. He walked over to the bookcases. He tilted his head to read the spines of the books. Then he drew closer with his enormous, potato-like nose and sniffed them. He walked away. He went over to the rickety old camp bed and sat down on the end of it. With his elbows on his knees and his face in his palms, he sighed again. His body was large, his face was large, his eyes were small. He was leaning forward, staring at a point somewhere between the desk and the bookcase. Was he looking at the coat stand, was that what he was looking at? He stayed there for a long time. He looked like he was chewing gum or a little piece of paper. Suddenly, something startled him. He sat bolt upright, listening intently, looking around. He stood up and left the room, then the house. I barely had time to hide behind the jasmine bush. I saw him walking away, heard his hurried footsteps. For a moment, as I saw him hop from the pavement to the street and cross the road, I suspected that perhaps the president wasn't as old as he'd like us to believe. After he'd disappeared, his footsteps lingered a while in the night. In the president's room, the light was still on.

I find it hard to believe that nobody in my house has noticed the president's visits yet. I'm starting to think my family have the right attitude. We must act as if the president has never visited us. But then I wonder: could he have come before without me knowing? No. He hasn't come before and my family don't know about his visits. They wouldn't be that good at pretending. But I'm really good at pretending. I can do it.

But then, who turned off the light in the president's room? I didn't dare. However, the next day, the light was off.

It isn't true that you can do it anywhere. You can't just whistle anywhere. Or you can, but then things change. Things rather than people, although sometimes people as well. On the way to school, while I'm whistling the tune I heard from the president, I can see how things I see every day, the same corners, the same houses, the same parked cars, the same trees, accept that this is also my voice. They accept me. It's uncomfortable and enjoyable at the same time. Although the tune has stayed in my head, I no longer dare to whistle it anywhere.

The idea that occurred to me behind the armchair, as I was watching the president sniff the air in the hallway and the house, was this: a little bag of dried lavender like the one my mother puts under her pillow to help her sleep better. That's what I want to put in the president's room. Tomorrow at breakfast I'll suggest it to our parents.

The thing with the little bag of lavender is something my grandmother used to do. She was the one who said it helped you sleep, and my mother just repeats it. I never knew her and neither did my big brother. Not even my father knew her. By the time they arrived in the house, there was just my grandfather with his fever and his shouting. Grandmother is therefore nothing but that single idea: a little bag of dried lavender to help you sleep. Grandmother is only there in the saying that my mother repeats. Once I thought of asking her what she meant by 'helping you sleep', but I never did. I'm scared that if I ask, the reply will dispel the scant presence of my grandmother. My grandmother is there, in that saying, and you can imagine her as the person in the family who sleeps the best.

We're all sitting round the table at breakfast. Nobody's talking and there's no sound save the clinking of coffee cups and cutlery. And the radio in the living room. As she does every morning, my mother's turned on the radio to hear the weather report. It's cold already. Suddenly it's cold. We're all there and I look at my family one by one. I want to tell them, to share my idea with them. My father, who's always the first to leave, is finishing his breakfast, so I need to hurry up. I have to say it. But then he goes and I don't say anything. Breakfast is finished and we all start to leave. It's not fear that stopped me from telling them. It's a kind of pride.

I was distracted all morning at school. But as soon as I got home I realised I'd made my decision: I was going to put the little bag of dried lavender in the president's room without telling anybody. During the siesta hour, I took some of the flowers my mother leaves to dry by the window and put them inside a sock, then I left them in my room and waited until night time. When everyone was asleep, I made my way downstairs barefoot and, without hesitation, opened the door of the president's room and went in. I didn't turn on the light. I stood in the darkness, observing the shadows. The desk, the coat stand, the bookcases, the camp bed, the side table with the bottle of whisky and the glass. Through the window, the black shadow of the laurel tree. Further away, the street light. It was the first time I'd ever been into that room on my own. Without anybody knowing. I'd never wanted to before. What was I doing here? Since when did I care about the president so much? But the president wasn't there. I put the sock full of dried lavender under the pillow and then turned and headed for the door, but I didn't leave. I stayed there in the darkness, my back to the closed door. Slowly, I made a mental list of all the objects I knew were in the room, those I could make out in the shadows and those I couldn't, the long-forgotten ones, the ones hidden away in drawers. I left space, on my list, for the objects I didn't know about. I thought of my father there, transformed into a stranger. Then I thought of the president, whistling his tune in the darkness. In the darkness, the camp bed looked too small for the president's body. There was no way he could fit on there, being so tall. And yet he had. I sniffed the air, I looked around. I smelt the scent of lavender but it was hard to tell if it was coming from the hidden sock or from my hands, which had touched it. I left the room.

In the attic. It's only in the attic, the part of the house that's furthest away from the president's room, that I can think clearly. It's been over a week since I left the sock full of dried lavender in there. The president hasn't returned and only in the attic can I think clearly about this, about all this. When I'm out of the house I think only of coming back, and the only way to stop thinking about coming back is to whistle the tune I heard from the president. When I'm at home, everything gets muddled. Even the bathrooms, the upstairs bathrooms, which were the beginning of everything and used to keep everything in order, no longer help. It's as if this house had a basement, although I know it doesn't. My brothers have started to notice that something's wrong with me, because I'm suddenly talking to them a lot. My little brother is sometimes delighted by this and sometimes suspicious. My big brother always looks at me as if some law of physics were playing out on my forehead.

So, is something wrong with me?

Two cloth handkerchiefs, normal scissors and nail scissors, several decks of cards, envelopes of various sizes, rubber bands, safety pins, a pocket knife with a corkscrew, blank notebooks and diaries, biros, fountain pens, coloured pencils, a pencil sharpener, matches, cigarettes, a battery-operated radio and spare batteries, a large coffee cup and a small coffee cup, packets of sugar, a comb, a book of crosswords, a box of teabags, an electric kettle, a large bottle of mineral water, some packets of sweet and savoury biscuits, a couple of tins of food (peas, lentils, tuna), books on science, biology and engineering, the little elephants, the magnifying glass, a small towel and a large towel, soap, shampoo, a basin, rock salt, a shoebox containing some medicines and bandages, a silk sleep mask, ear plugs, clocks, lots of clocks, some that work and some that don't, the revolver, the six bullets, the sock full of lavender. How long could the president survive in the room we've prepared for him?

It's impossible to know every single object that's in the president's room. And now I'm suspicious. As the days go by and I gradually lose hope that the president will return, I begin to suspect that I'm not the only one who's been into the room and left something without telling the others. We've cheated one another. We've been cheating one another. Would my mother have seen the sock full of dried lavender when she was cleaning the room? Would she have left it or taken it away? I need to go back into the president's room and have a look. But I can't find the right moment. I can't pluck up the courage. How did I do it before, how did I dare to go into the president's room like that? But above all, how did I dare to interfere with the order of the room?

I list the objects, the furniture, every time, as if I were taking them out of the room. I imagine taking them all out into the garden. I imagine the furniture and the objects in the afternoon sun, in the shade of the leafy laurel tree. There's light and shade at the same time, on the furniture, on the objects. Is there music in the air? Is it that music that comes from some place I don't know? I patiently list all the objects, but I never list the room. The empty room is something that suddenly I can no longer think about.

The president's fourth visit was on a very cold night. The president opened the front door with his key and came in. This time he was wearing a coat over his suit. An impeccable new overcoat, in a kind of black I'd never seen before. By the light of the hallway, in this overcoat, the president looked slimmer, his shoulders straight, held high. He smelled the air with his enormous nose, made a satisfied clicking sound at the warmth of the house and went into his room. I emerged from my hiding place behind the armchair and moved closer to the door he'd closed behind him. I pressed my ear against it and tried to hear what was going on. The president was whistling again. It was the same song but it sounded different. The light was on in the room. Despite the cold, I went out into the garden and hid by the jasmine bush under the window. I peered inside. The president was sitting in his recliner, and had poured himself a glass of whisky. He was still whistling quietly and hadn't taken off his overcoat. He looked relaxed, as if he had grown accustomed to the room. But if he had, he would have taken off his coat. He whistled and took the occasional sip of whisky. He remained in front of the window with his eyes closed for a long time. The cold was bearable, but the growing unease as the minutes passed was not. The president took sip after sip of whisky, very small sips, and each time, he grimaced so that his moustache twisted upwards, his forehead wrinkled and his nose expanded as if it were about to take over his whole face. The feeling of unease was linked to this: it was possible that the president didn't like whisky but he felt obliged to drink it. And he didn't just drink that glass, he also poured himself another. He drank the second glass with his eyes open. He was no longer whistling. He was looking out of the window, at the top of the laurel tree, at the night sky. His face was big, his nose was big and his eyes were small, until they began not to be small any more. His eyes were getting bigger, his eyebrows were raised, his eyes growing wide. Then the president stood up and came over to the window. I backed away and stumbled, falling onto the frozen grass. I saw him looking at the laurel tree and the black sky, and then suddenly his eyes were on me. But no: it wasn't sudden. His eyes had grown large and slow and several seconds passed as they looked down at me, at the moonlit grass. And then several more, and we didn't move. Him with his fixed stare and me staring back. Feeling the frost on my palms, wondering what his look meant. Until he finally turned around, left the empty glass next to the bottle and moved away from the window. A moment later, the light went out in the president's room. I heard the door to the room opening and closing and then the front door, and then the president appeared. Yes. He was tall and stooped. As I said. But it was as if I'd only just noticed. The president filled his lungs with the cold night air and his nose swelled in the shadows. Then he slowly exhaled. He crossed the garden path, reached the pavement, passed underneath the laurel tree and crossed the road. Only then did I stand up. He was tall and stooped. And as he walked away, he looked taller and more stooped, despite the new black overcoat. At no point did the president look at me. It was as if he'd never seen me before. But he had seen me. He had looked at me. With those big, slow eyes and that sad, malicious look. For a while I stood in the garden, shivering with cold. I couldn't make my mind up: the way the president looked at me, had it been the look of a good man, or a wicked man? Those were the only two options. Those were the only two options in those eyes, in the president's eyes.

I went back indoors. I went into the president's room. I lifted the pillow on the camp bed and checked that the sock full of dried lavender was still there. I lay down fully clothed and wrapped myself in the blanket. When the cold finally subsided, I slept. I slept until daybreak, when a musical whistling woke me. I thought the president had come back, but it was me. I could see the first light of day through the window. I thought about drawing the curtains, but I couldn't get up. Then I heard the first sounds of the house. My mother was up. And that's how it happened. Just like that, so simply, as I listened to the noises upstairs. The shuffling of my father's slippers. My little brother washing in the bathroom above my head. The sound of showers. A cough. One by one they were making their way downstairs, and I could tell who was who by their footsteps. They'd be making breakfast, my younger brother wouldn't have mentioned my absence yet, because he likes to hide those kinds of things. Now I was the one who'd disappeared. But it wouldn't last long. They'd find me easily enough. I was in the president's room and that's where I'd stay.

So there – here – I stayed.

At dawn, sometimes with the light off and sometimes with it on, I go to the window and let my eyes become large and slow. I look at the laurel tree, the black sky, the empty street. It's not that I'm waiting for the president, at least not always. With time, I'm getting used to the way things are, and I think about him less and less, just as my family think about me less and less. They accept me and I accept. We all accept. My mother goes on cleaning the room once a week and sometimes she pretends I am there, and others she pretends I'm not. I'm now part of the president's room. So what will happen when he comes? I don't know. I don't even know if he will come again. I don't think he will. But this doesn't worry me. It's no concern of mine. I'm just getting ready, making inventories and weaving relationships between the objects in the room. I play cards, I write, I read the science books left in here by my father, I teach myself, I imagine topics of conversation. It's not always easy. Sometimes I ask myself things. Will the girl I like carry on liking me, will she have noticed that I'm not at school? Sometimes I don't ask myself anything, but I still wonder. On those occasions, I go out into the garden and spy on the room again, through the window or from the laurel tree. On those days, when I come out of the bathroom under the stairs and pass by the staircase, I imagine going back to my room, to our room, which is now just my younger brother's room, and I sigh loudly, I sniff the air of the house. But that's only sometimes and they're not experiences that make an impression on me. Most of the time I'm happy. I'm happy and I'm occupied as my eyes become large and slow. Only every now and then, stretched out on the camp bed during the sun-filled siesta hour, do I desperately miss the attic. But that's only because, as people, we're always missing something.

CHARCO PRESS

Director/Editor: Carolina Orloff
Director: Samuel McDowell

www.charcopress.com

The President's Room was published on
80gsm Munken Print Cream paper.

The text was designed using Bembo 11 and ITC Galliard Pro.

Printed July 2017 by Bell and Bain Ltd.
303 Burnfield Road, Thornliebank, Glasgow G46 7UQ